ALIEN MY POCKET

POCKET

Blast Off!

ALIEN IN MY POCKET

Blast Off!

by
Nate Ball

illustrated by
Macky Pamintuan

HARPER
An Imprint of HarperCollinsPublishers

Alien in My Pocket: Blast Off
Copyright © 2014 by HarperCollins Publishers

Library of Congress Cataloging-in-Publication Data
Ball, Nate.
    Alien in my pocket / by Nate Ball ; [illustrated by Macky Pamintuan]. — First edition.
        pages   cm. — (Alien in my pocket)
    Summary: Fourth-grader Zack McGee's life is turned upside-down when Amp, a tiny
alien, crash-lands in his bedroom, then causes trouble at school while trying to get parts to
repair his spaceship.
    ISBN 978-0-06-221623-6 (pbk. bdg.)
    [1. Extraterrestrial beings—Fiction.   2. Friendship—Fiction.   3. Schools—Fiction.]   I.
Pamintuan, Macky, illustrator.   II. Title.
PZ7.B1989Ali 2014   2013003165
[Fic]—dc23   CIP
                                                                                        AC

Typography by Sean Boggs
13 14 15 16 17   OPM   10 9 8 7 6 5 4 3 2 1
❖
First Edition

Contents

01

Dream Invasion

There are times I think I might have that disease that makes people fall asleep right in the middle of doing something.

It's a real disease. I saw it on a TV show once. This guy who had the disease fell asleep while eating a bowl of cream of potato soup. *Splash!* Face first.

Once I fell asleep just *thinking* about spelling.

Anyway, the thought crossed my mind one night when I woke up with my face planted in a book. I had fallen asleep while studying for my first science quiz of the new school year.

You'd think static electricity would be the kind of subject that would interest a kid like me, but it wasn't. Not a spark of interest. Just sudden onset snoozing.

I jerked awake at my small, wobbly desk. My neck was stiff. My arm was numb. My mouth felt

3

like a bird had died in it.

Our house was eerily quiet. My little brother's room on the other side of the wall was silent. My parents had forgotten to say good night again. Both were trying to meet deadlines for "breakthrough experiments" and "research grants."

I switched off my little desk light. "That's enough studying for one night," I whispered in a croaky voice.

I lurched over to my window and pushed it open. From my second-story window, I had a good view of our dark and silent backyard. I sighed and leaned forward, my forehead against the screen. I guess I started to fall back asleep, because the next thing I knew the screen popped out of its frame and fell to the dim backyard below—and I nearly followed it down.

"Yipes," I whispered at the thought of spending fourth grade in a body cast.

My window screen had landed somewhere in the darkness, behind the bushes. At least I can lean out my window now, I thought.

I looked over at the house next to ours to see if Olivia's light was on. It wasn't.

Olivia has lived across the hedge from me pretty much forever. Our homes are so close that if the wind is blowing right she can fire a marshmallow with her marshmallow bazooka from her room and hit me in the face.

I was about to slide the window shut and collapse on my bed when I noticed a shooting star. A little good luck was just what I needed. I shut my eyes and quickly made a wish—actually three wishes at once: to finally make the travel baseball team, to get better grades, and to avoid detention all year. Why not make the most of the opportunity?

When I opened my eyes the falling star was still falling.

That's weird, I thought.

Falling stars usually last only half a second or so. But this one was streaking slowly from left to right across the night sky, heading toward the moon.

As I watched its flight, it looked like the falling star was falling slower—and getting bigger. I rubbed my eyes and leaned out my window as far as I could without falling out. The star *was* falling slower! And getting bigger!

I wondered for a second if this was one of Olivia's tricks. I looked over at her window again, but her entire house was dark and still.

I looked back into the night sky as the thing U-turned in my direction. It floated and weaved, a spray of orange and yellow sparks behind it.

This was *so* not a falling star.

And with a squeak of horror, I realized it was going to crash into my house.

In fact, it was going to crash into my bedroom!

I reached to slam my window shut, but before I could, the ball of fire lit up my backyard with sparks and flares and filled the neighborhood with a loud hissing sound.

I ducked—and just in time. The burning ball careened through the window.

It streaked over my head and thumped hard against the wall behind me.

The hissing sound stopped and was replaced by a grinding noise and then a quiet beeping sound.

My room was filled with smoke.

The lamp next to my bed had been knocked over.

There was a big, black burn mark above my bed and a basketball-size dent in the wall.

And resting on my comforter was a shiny, metal, football-shaped thing with little wings sticking out near one of the points. Steam sizzled out through tiny holes on either side and it continued to make a worrisome grinding noise. Like this: *GRUNK! GRUNK! GRUNK! GRUNK! GRUNK!*

I stared at it, wide-eyed, waiting for the thing to explode. I was too shocked to move.

You Are My Prisoner!

As the seconds passed, I realized the steaming, football-shaped thingy that had just landed on my bed was not going to blow up.

But what was it? A satellite? Part of a plane? A piece of the International Space Station?

I was about to bolt out of my bedroom door and scream my head off for my parents, for my little brother, for our dog, for our cat—but something stopped me.

Instead, I crawled over to my bed to get a closer look and came face-to-face with the shiny, football-shaped silver ball about the size of a barbecued chicken. Its gleaming skin seemed alive somehow. I could have reached out and touched it, but I didn't dare. It looked hot, and it was still making noises too weird to describe.

A loud click sounded, a tiny door sighed open, and a tiny set of stairs slowly folded down. Each step had a glowing strip of orange light, like in a dark movie theater.

And then a blue figure no bigger than my hand ducked his head out the door and stepped out onto the top of the stairs!

He coughed into his fist while waving the smoke away with his other hand.

I didn't know if I should laugh or scream. I felt stuck between amused and terrified—until I realized I hadn't thought to breathe in who knew how long.

I must have gasped or coughed. Or gasp-coughed. Because that's when it saw me. The little guy sank into a crouch and pulled a tiny remote control from the belt around his waist.

"Do not move, Earth person," he said in a squeaky, high-pitched voice.

He aimed his remote control at me. "I am Amp, lead scout from the plant Erde. According to the laws of Interplanetary Domination, you are now my prisoner!"

I think my reaction to this tiny guy's warning

had the opposite effect he was hoping for: I started cracking up. It was just hilarious. He wanted to sound tough and dangerous, but instead he sounded like a furious squirrel.

He didn't like my reaction. He aimed his remote control and fired at the tip of my nose. It felt like being zapped by static electricity—surprising, unpleasant, but not really painful. He growled in frustration, looked at his static gun, and then zapped me again.

"That hurts, you know," I told him, taking his zap gun away with two fingers.

"This is all wrong!" he squeaked in his funny

voice. "Why are you so big?"

"Uh, I don't know," I said, rubbing my nose. "Why are you so small?"

My response seemed to make him even more frustrated. He snatched the helmet off his head and flung it at me with a grunt. Smaller than half an eggshell, it bounced off my chest and fell silently to the carpet.

I noticed each of his hands had only a thumb and two chubby fingers.

Not thinking, I picked him up by the collar. He kicked and waved his arms crazily. He was really soft and warm, the way I imagine a hamster would feel if you shaved it and painted it blue.

"What are you?" I

asked. "Where did you come from, little guy?"

"I am not a little guy, and I am not from around here," he announced in his funny high-pitched voice. "And I am very dangerous."

And before I could stop him, he bit my finger.

I dropped him onto my bed, and he bounced away. I lunged for him, but he jumped off my bed before my hand could close around him.

I couldn't let him get away!

But by the time I made it around my bed, he had climbed up my chair and jumped onto my desk, and he was heading toward my open window.

With one last desperate leap, I dove for him just as he leaped up and out my window—and into the darkness below.

Hey, You!

What had I done?

For a moment, I stared into the blackness below my window, searching for any sign of the tiny visitor. I wanted to call out his name, but I had forgotten what it was!

I leaned out my window and whispered in desperation, "Hello? Can you hear me, Tramp? Or was it Stamp? Lamp? Cramp? Oh, what the heck is your name?"

No answer.

I started to panic and shouted in frustration, "Little blue dude, where'd you go?"

I'd let an alien escape from my room! Mankind would want to ground me for eternity!

I couldn't even remember the planet he said he was from. Was it Fergie? Murky? I should have paid attention. Why couldn't I ever pay attention?!?

I bolted to my door and, taking a deep breath, opened it slowly and quietly. I so didn't want to wake my family. Once there was enough space to squeeze through, I took off down the dark hallway, not aware that one of my brother's robots had parked itself just outside my room.

I tripped over it, of course, and went sprawling onto the carpet, flipping the robot onto its back like a helpless tortoise. Its motor sprang to life, its wheels started spinning crazily, and its headlights lit up the carpet at a crazy angle.

I held my breath for a moment—and amazingly, no one woke up.

I picked the robot up and used its headlights to make my way downstairs. I saw the light was on in my parents' office as I headed toward the back door. I tried to be careful to make sure they hadn't seen me, but while looking back over my shoulder I ran into the entryway table, knocking a bowl full of keys and change on the floor!

My future as a burglar did not seem bright.

With no time to spare I crept out the front door and closed it quietly behind me.

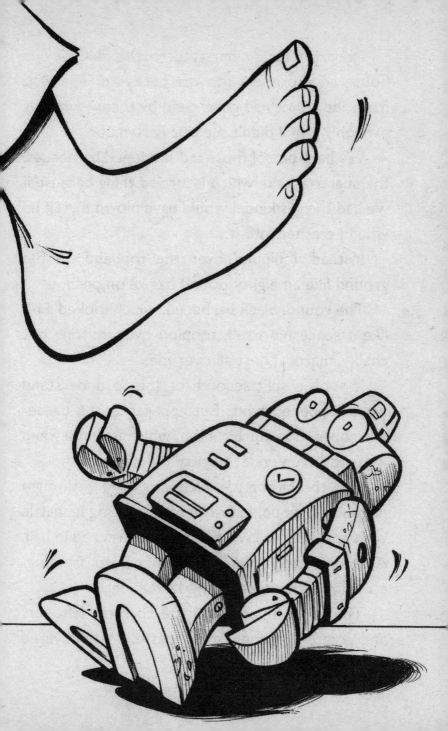

I burst through the gate to the side of our house and sprinted into the backyard. The light from the robot had gone dead by then—which is probably why I didn't see our barbecue.

We have one of those old-fashioned barbecues, the charcoal kind, which is a good thing because if we had the gas kind, I would have blown myself up when I crashed into it.

Instead, I flipped over the top and hit the ground like an eighty-pound bag of onions.

The round, black barbecue, which looked a bit like a spaceship itself, toppled over, spitting out chalky charcoal dust all over me.

It took a split second for me to understand what happened next. But apparently the barbecue rolled into our birdbath, which is wobbly and unsteady even under normal conditions.

And the birdbath, which was filled with dirty bird water, wobbled briefly before losing its battle with gravity. It fell with a thud and cracked in half. A second later, a wave of feather-filled, freezing-cold birdbath water washed over me.

The water mixed with the charcoal leftovers and created a gooey, sticky paste. I was covered in it. As I tried to get up, I slipped and slid over our patio like a first-time ice skater.

As if to add to my misery, Olivia's bedroom light snapped on then. "You have got to be kidding me," I growled.

As her curtain pulled back, I stumbled behind our doghouse. Thank goodness Smokey now slept in the garage. He was a barker.

I did not have time to explain to Olivia why I was covered in gray paste and making enough noise to wake up half the neighborhood.

I had to find Shemp—or whatever his dang

name was—before he got away!

Wiping barbecue dust out of my ears, I thought I heard something.

I froze and listened until I heard it again, and then I strained and listened even harder to figure out where the sound was coming from.

But instead of the alien, I heard Olivia's window slide open. "Zack, are you out there?"

I didn't answer. I listened so hard for the sound I'd heard I thought my ears would fall off my head.

"Help!" I heard.

The sound was so high, it was easy to think it was just my imagination.

It wasn't.

I crawled on my hands and knees around the back of the doghouse and came face-to-face with Mr. Jinxy, our fat cat.

He had the blue guy pinned to the wall of the doghouse with a paw. He was playing with him, like some kind of blue mouse.

"Go find a real mouse, Mr. Jinxy," I said, gently pushing him away from Amp.

I snatched up the tiny man. "Sorry about that," I said quietly. "You okay?"

"What was that thing?" he squeaked from my hand.

"It's a cat," I said. "Cats are animals. People have them because . . . Well, people like to have cats because . . . Actually I don't like cats, and I have no idea why we even have one."

The blue guy stared at me for a long time. "Oh, well, that clears things up."

I tiptoed in my squishy socks to our back door in relief.

"I knew it was you!" I heard Olivia call out from her open window. I'd completely forgotten about her. "What are you up to, Zack McGee?"

By this point, I was too exhausted for questions. I pretended not to hear and closed the door behind me. I knew I'd have a lot of explaining to do at the bus stop in the morning.

Busted!

I held what may have been the most amazing scientific discovery in the history of discovering stuff.

I was also soaked and covered in cold barbecue goo.

I tiptoed past my parents' office to the laundry room. I pulled off my soaked, lumpy socks and gray, goo-covered pants. Not an easy thing to do while holding a tiny blue creature. I dropped my clothes into the laundry basket and covered the mess with a clean towel.

He seemed to be looking at me in utter amazement, too.

"Haven't you ever seen someone get undressed?" I whispered before noticing he didn't wear socks, pants, or any clothes whatsoever. He only had a belt full of little compartments like a handyman's and a kind of backpack thing. "Just curious, are you a boy or girl?" I thought to ask.

"I don't understand," he said after a moment.

"Are you a boy whatever you are or a girl one?"

"I do not know what you're talking about, earthling," he said.

"Call me Zack," I said in a friendly voice.

"I still do not know what you're talking about, Zack," he said.

"What's your name again? I forgot."

He looked at me for a full ten seconds before answering. "It's Amp."

"Uh . . . Amp, where are your clothes?"

"Clothes? We Erdians are an advanced civilization and we can regulate our body temperature without clothes, thank you," he said. "Tell me this: Why do you wear clothes, but your Mr. Jinxy does not?"

"What? Cats don't wear clothes," I exclaimed. "That's ridiculous."

"Interesting," he said, and then he whispered into his wristband:

**"Council Note: Human creatures
are warm-blooded. They have a
constant body temperature—but
they insist on wearing clothes.
Investigate further."**

"What was that?"

"What?"

"That thing you just did."

"Notes for the Erde Council."

"The Erde Council?"

"Erde is what we call my planet," he said, shaking his head in frustration. "I already told you that. The Council is our supreme leaders. You are not a good listener, Zack McGee."

"That's what my teacher says," I said with a smile. He didn't smile back. He looked rather annoyed. "I'm not going to eat you, you know," I explained.

"Thanks for that," he said, throwing his arms up in frustration.

I shrugged. "You're kinda moody, you know that?"

"You're kinda moody, you know that?" he said back, imitating me.

"Be quiet now," I whispered.

"You be quiet now!" he squeaked angrily as I stepped out into the kitchen and skittered toward the stairs in my bare feet.

Light suddenly filled the hallway and I froze. "What's going on, Zack?" It was my dad. He was standing in the doorway to his office.

I slowly dropped the hand holding the Erdian guy to my side, like I was sneaking a cookie. "Nothing. Why?"

"Why?" he asked, puzzled. "Well, because it's two hours past your bedtime and you're running around the house in your underwear."

I looked down, trying to come up with a reason for not wearing pants. "My pajamas are around here somewhere," I said lamely, looking around.

"I heard a loud thump earlier and a big bang just a minute ago. What's going on?"

I could feel Amp squirming, but I didn't dare reveal my hidden hand.

I gulped. "Uh . . . My pants were muddy, so I left them in the laundry room for Mom."

"How'd your pants get muddy?"

"Good question," I said, trying to think of

some good excuses for my weird behavior. I came up with nothing.

"Go to bed, Zack," he moaned. "You've got school tomorrow."

"Okay," I peeped, then shot up the stairs, zipped down the hallway, and closed my door quietly behind me.

It had flashed through my mind that I should tell my dad, but I just couldn't share my secret, not just yet. This was *my* discovery. Everybody in my house was a science big shot. Maybe now *I* would be the big shot, too. Images of me and my alien on the covers of magazines flashed through my mind: "Science Whiz Kid Captures Blue Alien!"

"I can't breathe!" the creature wheezed from between my fingers.

"Oh, sorry," I said. "Must be all the excitement."

He gulped for air. "That earthling was even bigger than you!" he said with tiny, wide eyes. "My size charts are all wrong."

"That's my dad," I explained. "I'm just a kid. I'm pretty small, actually, but I'll grow bigger."

"Blast!" he said, pounding his little fist into the palm of his other hand. "Our calculations were way off. This is a disaster!"

"What's a disaster?"

"You're much too big for what we were planning," he said, distracted.

"Don't worry, little man, I'll take care of you."

"You don't understand!" he shouted, grabbing his forehead with both hands.

I laughed at his high voice, which sounded extra funny when he was mad.

"Why are you laughing? This is an intergalactic snafu of epic proportions!"

"I'm not even sure what that means," I said.

"I need to get back to Erde and call off the attack," he said, looking over at his now-quiet spaceship.

"You can't leave!" I cried. "You just got here! I've got to show you off. Maybe enter you in the science fair. We can be on magazine covers."

"No, you want me to leave, trust me," he said. "And you can't tell anybody about me."

"Oh, come on, you don't strike me as the shy type. We could be on TV!"

"If your leaders learn of me, I'll never get home in time," he squeaked.

29

"Relax, I'll take care of you. I'll be your agent. Cool?"

"What's an agent?" he said, suddenly concerned.

"You know," I said, trying to figure out what I was talking about. "For movies, TV shows, comic books. Hey, can you sing?"

"I don't know what you're talking about, Zack!"

"We'll be famous."

"We don't have time to be famous. You have to help me repair that," he said, pointing at his spaceship.

"Me?" I said. "I've never fixed a thing in my life! And besides, my wall didn't hit you, you hit my wall!"

"What do you know about repairing an initial launch system?" he asked.

"Not a single thing. Breaking things is more my specialty."

"Not anymore," he said with a nod. "If we don't fix my ship, the entire Erdian army is going to invade Earth."

I knew he was right. I had to help. If one of him could cause this much trouble, a whole army of Amps would probably get me grounded for life.

Morning

Sunlight woke me up. It was that kind of extra-bright sunrise light that digs under your eyelids and kicks your eyeballs around in their sockets.

And the chilly morning air in my room wrapped itself around me.

I had forgotten to close my window. And my curtains.

I hadn't even gotten under the covers.

As my mind slowly became aware of these things, I thought of the alien. Amp.

What a dream! It was all so real.

The details danced through my sleepy mind. Amp had told me all about his planet. He told me he was a scout, sent to study humans and Earth and to confirm that this would be a good planet for his people to invade. He told me about

learning our language from studying TV show signals they'd found in space. He even described his broken spaceship and its ability to skip through enormous stretches of space in an instant—like a stone skipping over water.

The backyard sprinklers popped to life then. It was an hour earlier than I needed to be up. I closed my eyes, wishing for a few more minutes of sleep, when a bumping sound caught my attention. Then a bigger, louder bump. And then: Olivia.

"Nice boxers, Zack," she said, though her voice sounded far away.

I sat up wearily and croaked when I saw the giant burn mark on the wall above my bed—the one made by Amp's spaceship!

IT WAS ALL TRUE?

IT ALL REALLY HAPPENED!

My brain locked up.

"Baseballs, bats, and gloves," I heard Olivia say again. "Such a cute pattern for your unmentionables."

Unmentionables? That's what Olivia called underwear. Unmentionables! But where was her voice coming from?

Just outside my window bobbed a cardboard tube. A cardboard tube? I shook my head and croaked for the second time. Olivia was in my backyard, looking through my window with a periscope she made last summer. And she could see me in my boxers!

Agh!

"Is that a Smurf?" her voice called up from below.

I gasped. Amp was standing absolutely still in front of my alarm clock. Without moving his head, his eyes darted over at me. "What is that talking tube?" he said, barely moving his lips. "What do I do?"

I'd like to say I think quickly in an emergency, like one of those slick spy guys in the movies. But apparently I don't. I just kept looking back and forth from Amp to the periscope, waiting for something to happen.

"You know your window's screen is down here?" Olivia said from the backyard below. "I accidentally stepped on it. It's a little bent. . . . Sorry."

The periscope tilted and floated at an odd angle. Olivia was clearly looking at my screen. I took the opportunity to jump off my bed and pull my curtains closed.

Poking my head through the curtains, I looked down at Olivia. "Do you mind, Olivia? Total invasion of privacy!"

"Oh, sorry," she said, clearly surprised by the emotion in my voice. "I saw your window was open and figured you were awake. Sorry I saw your unmentionables. I won't tell anyone, I swear."

"They're not unmentionables. They're boxers!"

"I was just kidding," she said.

Now I felt bad. "It's just . . ."

"Where'd you get that blue doll? That's new, right?"

"Blue doll?"

"The blue elf thing?" she asked. "Is that what you were playing with last night?"

"Oh, that," I said, poking my head farther out of my curtain like some kind of weird, one-headed puppet show. "It's . . . uh . . . it's kind of a long story."

35

"Okay," she said lowering her periscope. "This was a bad idea."

"It's okay," I said. "We'll talk later," I said, needing to end this conversation and deal with the mess in my room.

I closed the curtains and looked at Amp. "We have some work to do."

"You're right, Zack," he nodded crisply. "We need to fix my spaceship right away, starting with the launch system"

"Fix your spaceship? I have to go to school! I

was talking about cleaning up my room before my parents see it. "

"Oh," he said, looking around my room. "Good luck."

"'Good luck'?" I yelped, narrowing my eyes at him. "Oh, great, the alien who destroyed my room with a bad parking job doesn't like cleaning up after himself."

He shrugged and smiled weakly. "That's not really my thing."

It occurred to me then that having a wise guy alien around was going to be a lot harder than I thought.

06

Frozen Waffles (Again)

I plopped down for my breakfast with Amp hiding in my room upstairs. I felt sick, scared, tired, excited, smart, stupid, thrilled, horrified, hungry, stuffed, happy, sad, grumpy, dizzy, and halfway crazy—all at the same time.

My mom kept feeling my forehead and neck as I nibbled at the edges of my frozen waffle. I had forgotten to toast it. She was pretty sure I was coming down with something.

"Zack, you look like you didn't sleep a wink," she said, taking the frozen waffle from me and dropping it into the toaster. "Somebody was snooping around last night, leaving footprints everywhere." She gave me "the look."

"It was Zack," my dad said, giving me a glance over his coffee cup. "I caught him wandering

around the house in his boxers last night."

"Maybe he's in love," my little brother Taylor said, stabbing his Pop-Tart with an annoying electric fork he had invented. "With Olivia."

My dad shook his bacon at me. "Remember, Zack, you promised to change your tune this year. Hit the books."

"He hit the books, all right," my brother said. "I peeked in his room last night and he was using his science book for a pillow. He's a drooler."

"And you're a snooper," I growled.

Dad cleared his throat. "Zack, fourth grade is going to be the year you turn things around, right? We talked about this."

"Dancing around in his underwear doesn't sound very focused to me," Taylor said, staring at his stupid fork.

"Enough," Dad said to Taylor, who could never take a hint.

"I can tutor Zack in science," he offered sweetly. "Free of charge."

"And I can tutor your face. Free of charge," I said. Taylor is a science geek and a show-off. He brags about liking science more than PE, which is clearly abnormal.

Dad gave us his glare. "Can it," he said.

"Zack, you look like a zombie," Mom said. She handed me my toasted waffle and shoved her entire arm down the back of my shirt, searching desperately for any sign of a fever.

"I just had some weird dreams," I mumbled.

"Which explains why you were sleepwalking in your underwear," Taylor teased.

Normally, I would have threatened to pound him so hard his grandchildren would walk with a limp. But now, I just stared at him.

My parents exchanged another look.

I stuck a finger into my mango-orange-pineapple juice and stuck it in my mouth. I couldn't taste a thing. It was becoming clear to me that keeping Amp a secret was going to be near impossible.

I already felt strangely protective of Amp. I didn't want him taken away forever by grown-ups. If the government swooped in, they'd take him away to some secret lab somewhere to do tests. I knew how things worked—my parents

41

are scientists, after all—and what some goofy ten-year-old kid wanted to do with his alien visitor wouldn't be worth doodley-squat.

I needed to stick with my plan for now. I'd get through the school day, return here immediately after, and then figure out how best to deal with the alien babysitting my goldfish. Maybe I could introduce him to Olivia, or my parents. I'd have to hash this out with Amp, but it was clear that I alone couldn't fix his spaceship. I was going to need help, and I'd have to explain this to Amp.

"Maybe you should stay home, dear," Mom said, hands fluttering on her hips.

"He's fine," Dad said, not looking up from his smartphone.

"He always looks like that," Taylor said. "Snap out of it, boxer boy. The bus is coming in four minutes."

As we gathered up our things for our final inspection at the door, Mom gave me a worried once-over. "If you don't feel well, go to the office and have Miss Sturney call me on my cell phone."

"I will," I said with a weak smile.

As Taylor and I crossed the front lawn I looked back at the house, feeling like I was making a big mistake by leaving Amp alone.

07

Bus Breakdown

Olivia tried to get in all sorts of questions before the bus arrived. But the great thing about always running late is that I barely had time to tell her I was feeling "a bit off" before the bus pulled up.

The best seats were already taken when we got on. I had to squeeze into a seat way in the back of the bus. I didn't see Max Myers get on at the next stop until it was too late—which is pretty startling, considering Max is as big as the bus driver and I think he's already started shaving.

Max pitches on the travel baseball team, the one I want to earn a spot on. But I'm a catcher, and just the thought of catching fastballs thrown by Max Myers makes me want to forget baseball and take up lawn darts.

"McGee, you're forgetting the Max Factor," he said.

"Really?" I said, wishing that the bus driver would tell Max to sit down, but nobody tells Max to do much of anything.

"Don't be smart, McGeek," he said.

Usually Olivia can outthink Max and send him on his way, but she had to sit up front. Taylor was up there somewhere, too, with the first graders. I was all on my own. "Sorry, Max, I'm not sure what you're talking about."

"It's Mr. Max to you, McGeek," he bellowed.

The bus went quiet. Everybody turned around to see what the commotion was. My guts went cold.

"Max Factor," he repeated. "You know I get the rear seat all to myself. You're cruising for a bruising," he said, grabbing me by the shirt collar.

"Oh," I said weakly, looking for an empty seat nearby. Of course, there were none.

That's when something unexpected happened.

"I love you like a brother, McGee," Max roared with real emotion in his eyes. He let me go and seemed puzzled, like he couldn't remember why he said this. "I want you to be, like, my BFF, Zack!"

This comment drew gasps from the stunned crowd. Max doesn't have friends. He has minions.

I smiled weakly. "That's cool, Mr. Max," I managed to say.

"Here, take my lunch money," he said, suddenly pulling two dollars out of his pocket and thrusting them at my face.

All I could think was that this must be some kind of a trick. "That's okay, Mr. Max. You need to eat."

That's when movement in my backpack caught my eye. I looked down and saw Amp poking his head out of the zipper in my backpack's small pen-and-pencil pocket. My mouth dropped open. My mind spun. He must have snuck in this morning when I wasn't looking. I had an alien stowaway in my backpack!

47

Amp was holding both hands over his mouth, like he was holding back a laugh. I was too stunned to think.

"Oh my gosh, I smell roses!" Max hollered. "Can anybody smell that? I love the smell of flowers in the morning!" Max was almost crying with excitement, but all I could smell was a stale, dirty bus. If I thought the bus was quiet before, it was now pin-drop silent.

My eyes darted back down at Amp, who seemed to be having the time of his life.

That's when I realized that Amp was doing all this to Max! He was making Max say these things, which is why Max seemed so utterly shocked by his own words. I shook my head at Amp. "No," I whispered, "you'll get caught."

"I NEED TO ITCH MY BACK!" Max hooted at the top of his lungs. "AGH!" He dropped his backpack and bent his body every which way, trying to scratch his itch. "I can't reach it," he squealed.

To everyone's utter amazement, Max dropped to all fours in the aisle of the bus. "SCRATCH!" he thundered and several kids snapped out of their trance and scratched Max's big, bulky back.

Max moaned with delight. "So good," he sang over and over.

It was one of the weirdest scenes any of us had ever witnessed. It was so odd that it was even more troubling than being threatened by Max Myers himself. I had never understood what the word "unsettling" meant until that moment. It was unsettling to see someone like Max act so odd and crazy.

But it was kind of funny, too.

Amp knew how to make people do stuff. How cool was that?

The possibilities raced through my mind: I could get straight A's now. Make the travel baseball team. Ask my mom to raise my allowance . . . and she'd have to say yes.

Fourth grade was going to be more interesting than I ever imagined.

The Plan?

"**W**hat happened to the plan?" I said into my backpack as I snuck into an empty science lab to talk to Amp before first bell.

"What plan?" Amp said innocently in his squeaky voice.

"Nice advanced civilization," I grumbled. "You can't even stay put for ten minutes."

"Look who's talking about civilizations," he said, pointing at me from the pocket. "My civilization doesn't create ploogs like Max Myers."

"'Ploog'?" I yelped. "What's a ploog?"

"It's Erdian—and I'm not telling you what it means. You're not old enough."

"Really? And how old are you?"

"Hmmm. If you wanted to count my age by your solar calendar—ours is totally different, of course—with each rotation of Earth around your sun being equal to one year . . . I'm about 412."

"Seriously? Amp, you're a total geezer!"

"Don't get ploogy on me now, Zack McGee," he said.

"Okay, I call a truce," I said, putting my back-pack down on a lab worktable. "I thought we agreed you'd stay hidden in my room until I got home this afternoon."

"I'm a scout," he explained simply, "so you can understand how I'd be a little bit curious to learn more

about Earth." He stepped out of the pocket and surveyed the science classroom.

"*That's* your periodic table of the elements?" he guffawed, pointing to a big chart on the wall. He studied it for a minute. "Zack, you're missing over half of the elements!"

"Amp, I don't even know what an element is," I said simply.

Amp sighed and then turned his back and whispered into his wrist:

"Council Note: Earthlings have only identified 118 elements. They have organized them by something called an atomic number."

Then he looked over his shoulder at me and shrugged. "I went to school for over a hundred Earth years, you know."

"Whoa, and I thought I had it bad."

The first bell rang then. It almost scared the blue off of Amp. He dove back into the pocket headfirst. Man, he was fast when he wanted to be.

"What on Erde was that?" he called out from

somewhere in the pocket.

"Just first bell," I groaned. I pressed the top of my head with both hands, trying to think. "You can't bring a hamster to school without three permission slips. I can't imagine what they'd think about a four-hundred-year-old alien."

"They'd probably make an exception," Amp said hopefully, crawling back out of the backpack.

"No!" I snapped. "Principal Luntz makes no exceptions. He has a strict no-exceptions policy. Of course, I don't think the Reed School Student Conduct Guidebook covers alien invaders."

"I can handle the principal," he said. "Just bring me to him and I'll have him barking like a cat in no time."

"That's not gonna happen," I said. "And cats don't bark; dogs bark." His threat reminded me of the bus trip and Max Myers. "Now explain what happened with that ploog Max Myers."

"Ploog?" Amp shouted with delight. "You learn things fast, Zack."

"How'd you make him do those things?" I asked. "It's like the most awesome Jedi mind trick ever! Can you teach me how to do that?"

"No, I can't," he said. "My brain is different from yours."

"Yeah, it's probably the size of a peanut."

"Smaller, yes, but much more dense."

"You're dense?" I asked. "I think that means dumb."

"No, as in density!" Amp said with disbelief. "C'mon, Zack, density is the ratio of mass to volume, a measurement of compactness. You should know that by now."

"Oh, right. But what's that got to do with mind tricks?"

"Let's see, how can I explain this?" Amp stared at the ceiling for a second, then continued. "I can send a quick pulse, a short mental burst, similar to a sound wave, that can impact a human brain's thoughts, but just for a few seconds. It's more like an impulse."

"An impulse?" I asked.

"You seem somewhat unfamiliar with your own language. Haven't you read your dictionaries and encyclopedias? An impulse is a strong and sudden urge to act or do something, but it doesn't last."

"That's why Max went from being my best friend, to offering me his lunch money, to smelling flowers, to having an itch," I said excitedly, getting it now.

"Exactly," Amp said. "It's powerful, but it doesn't last."

"Do me!" I exclaimed, clapping at the thought of it. "C'mon, try one on me."

"Really? Are you sure?" Amp asked. I nodded. "Okay," he said with a smile.

Suddenly, I could taste the worst sour milk imaginable. Not just a few days old, but a few weeks old—the kind of spoiled, curdled milk with the big, slimy, gray blobs in it. "AUGH!" I rasped, ready to puke up my half-eaten frozen waffle.

I proceeded to stumble around gagging for a few seconds and, just like Amp said, it faded as fast as it came on. Powerful, but brief. My breakfast was safe, for now.

"You couldn't make me taste cherry pie? Or pizza? You had to do sour milk?" I shouted.

"I was looking for a powerful demonstration," he chirped with delight. "Now that I have your attention, there may be some materials here that we'll need for fixing my ship. Do they have strong magnets in a classroom like this? How about tungsten?"

"What in the world is tungsten?"

"It's right there in the table of elements, the box with the big W," he said, pointing at the poster on the wall. "Its atomic number is seventy-four,

which tells us how many protons are in its nucleus. Tungsten is a very dense metal with an extremely high melting point—the second highest of your elements, after carbon, of course. We'll need some of that if we are going to repair my ship."

"Man, you're a total nerd, Amp," I sighed.

"And you're more dense than I thought," he said with a shake of his head. "So do they have any here?"

"Amp, this is the science lab, and this year is the first year I'll get to come in here, but I haven't had a science lab yet. So I don't know if they have your tongue stuff."

"Tungsten," he corrected.

"Whatever," I replied. "Plus, I've got to go to class."

"Then I'll just stay here," he waved at me. "Go on and learn, I'll stay here and survey the inventory."

"Oh no, you won't," I said forcefully. "I'm not leaving you anywhere. You'll get caught."

"Nobody will catch me, Zack, we need to gather these materials now to—"

The second bell rang. Amp yelped and bolted

back inside his pocket with the pens and pencils. "How often does that floofy noise happen?" he called out with irritation.

"'Floofy?' Speak English, please," I said, snatching up my backpack, zipping Amp's pocket closed, and heading for the door. "That's the second bell. It means I have less than a minute to be in my seat."

09

Classroom Commotion

Rule #1: If you ever have an alien, do not bring it to school.

Ever.

Aliens and school do not mix.

This became clear within a few minutes after collapsing in my chair at the front of my classroom.

"Oh dear, does anyone smell vanilla?" Miss Martin was asking by the time I stuffed my backpack under my chair. She laughed nervously. "It's like a vanilla extract truck has tipped over," she said, looking out the window. "It's so strong."

"Oh, no," I whispered to myself. "Not again."

The entire class was silent, looking puzzled and giving each other mystified looks and shrugs.

"Class, please open up your social studies workbooks to chapter seventeen," Miss Martin

59

commanded as she returned to her senses. Before I could pull my workbook out she made another odd announcement. "First, class, I'd like everyone to know that I think Zack McGee is this school's most handsome young man," she said with oddly questioning eyes.

After a moment of stunned silence, everybody erupted in laughter. I sank lower in my chair. My face got warm.

"Amp," I thought with all my might. "Please stop! Please don't do this!"

Suddenly, Emily Binkbarton stood up next to her desk and exclaimed, "Oh, I agree, Miss Martin. He's as cute as peaches."

Peaches?

The class erupted with more laughter.

"Zack's face makes me feel safe and relaxed," shouted Davey Swope, apparently horrified by his own mouth.

Safe and relaxed? What the—

"I want to run my fingers through his hair!" Lexie Evans suddenly blurted out, as if she just won the big prize at bingo.

Now the laughter was so out of control it

seemed to fill my head.

I must have blushed bright red. My face felt like it was about burst into flames.

Amid all this laughing, commotion, and confusion, I whipped my backpack out from under my desk, dropped it roughly on my desk, and yanked open the zipper of the pen-and-pencil pocket.

"Amp, you cannot just—" I began.

The pocket was empty.

Huh?

Amp was gone.

"Amp!" I yelped, searching desperately around my desk.

My alien had gone rogue!

"What is going on?" Olivia said in my ear, her voice piercing through the roar around us. Olivia sits a few desks behind me, in my row, but she was now standing next to me, shaking my shoulder. "Is this a prank? It's great. Why didn't you tell me?"

"I can't talk right now," I said, pushing past her. With my backpack clutched in my hand, I proceeded to squat down and duckwalk down the aisle, searching furiously around everyone's feet.

"Amp!" I growled. "You're in big trouble, mister. I'm gonna wring that tiny blue neck of yours! Get back in your pocket!"

He was nowhere.

"Zack McGee, please take your seat," Miss Martin ordered from behind me with a loud clap. Her impulse about my handsomeness had apparently faded. In fact, everyone else seemed back to normal, too. Amp probably was no longer in the room. Then it occurred to me: all this crazy talk was just a distraction. Amp used his Jedi mind trick so he could escape! He was probably running wild through the hallways right now looking for the science lab and his tongue stuff.

"Can I go to the bathroom?" I asked abruptly, jumping to my feet.

She must have seen the absolute panic in my eye. "By all means, Zack," Miss Martin said with an understanding nod, waving me toward the door.

I stumbled out into the deserted hallway. Where was he? "I'm getting you a cage!" I whispered as loudly as I could.

I figured he was headed for the lab, so I bolted around the corner and ran right into Principal

Luntz. His big belly stopped me like a wall of cheese.

"McGee, this is not good," he said, staring down at me. He took a firm hold of my arm. With his other hand he poked his glasses back up his nose. He shook his head with disappointment. "Why are you running through the halls during class? What's going on?"

Never before had telling the truth seemed like less of an option.

"Let's see if a call to your parents loosens your tongue," he huffed in frustration, walking me toward the school office.

10

Principal Luntz

"What is going on with you?" Olivia said. Olivia?

She sat down next to me on one of the chairs lined up outside Principal Luntz's office. I was waiting to be called in. She proceeded to punch me in the arm—not hard, but hard enough to let me know she wasn't happy about being left out.

"What are you doing here?" I asked, looking around. "How'd you get out of class? Did you see anything odd in the hallway?"

"I got a bathroom pass," she replied simply, jumping up and pressing her ear to the frosted glass on Principal Luntz's door.

"Get away from there," I hissed. "You're going to get busted."

"You're acting like a weirdo," she said, narrowing

her eyes at me. She sat back down in the chair next to mine. "You're sleeping with your window wide open so the whole world can see your unmentionables. You're acting funny at the bus stop. You've got Max Myers crawling on the bus. You're pulling off class pranks. Now you're tangling with Principal Dunce."

"It's Luntz, not Dunce," I whispered. "Be quiet, will you? I'm in enough trouble already."

She placed her hand on my forehead.

PR

"Maybe you caught some kind of insanity flu. Do you feel hot?"

I pushed her hand away. "It's not like that. It's kind of complicated."

"Look who you're talking to! I'm a complicated chick. Spill the beans, Zacky."

"I'm in a situation here," I said. "It's best if you avoid getting tangled up in my web of disaster."

"Look, I'm a fixer, right?" she said, raising her eyebrows at me. "You've got a problem; I can fix it. I can handle Luntz," she said, jumping to her feet. "Let me speak on your behalf," she assured me, reaching out for the doorknob to Luntz's office.

"Wait!" I pleaded. "Okay! Okay! I can sort of tell you what's going on, but only because I may need your help finding my . . . my . . . new friend."

Olivia looked at me with a funny face. "New friend? Do tell, Zack McGee."

I collected my thoughts before speaking. "I have sort of a houseguest. A secret houseguest."

She looked at me like a weasel just crawled out of my nose. "You mean at your house-home? Where you live?"

"Yes! You don't know him. He's really . . . um . . . really short."

"You have a secret short man living at your house? Is he your Uncle Herb?"

"No, no! You've never met him. He's not from around here."

"So, you've got a short stranger living in your house?" she said slowly. She stared off for a few moments. "What's that got to do with Miss Martin smelling vanilla or thinking you're hot stuff?"

"Well, this guest . . . He's different," I said, trying not to say too much. "He's . . . well, he's blue."

"Blue? You mean, he's really sad?"

I knew this wasn't going to be easy. "No, not that kind of blue," I groaned. "You're not getting it."

"Oh, I think I am!" she said, raising her voice now. "You've got a secret, really short, very blue man who isn't from around here living at your house. That makes perfect sense!"

"He's actually not a man," I said, sinking lower into my chair. "He says he's not a boy or a girl. He is both and neither at the same time."

Olivia stared at me for a full minute. "Zack McGee, you are too old for imaginary friends."

69

"He's not imaginary," I hissed.

"What's wrong with you?" Olivia shouted. She grabbed my shoulders with both hands and shook me vigorously. "Snap out of it!"

"MCGEE, WHAT'S GOING ON OUT HERE?!"

Principal Luntz had thrown open his office door. His face was red and unhappy.

Olivia suddenly stood up and brushed the wrinkles out of her shirt, composing herself like a professional actor. "Sir, I am here to represent the best interests of one Zack McGee, the troubled youth you see sitting here before you."

If I'd sunk any lower in my chair, I'd have been on the floor.

Luntz looked us both over for what seemed like an eternity. "Fine, but I'll talk to you separately. You first," he said, pointing to Olivia.

I jumped up to protest, but he gave me his extremely-serious-principal look, and I slowly slumped back into my chair.

As his door clicked closed, I considered the fact that I should have listened to my mom and stayed home today.

11

Friends in High Places

As I listened to Olivia's muffled voice behind the glass of Principal Luntz's office, I considered the mess my life had become. My "new start" in fourth grade seemed in total jeopardy.

"I'm sorry, Zack," Amp's voice said from the chair next to me.

"AAGH!" I yelped, nearly leaping out of my own skin. "Where'd you come from?"

"Oh, please, I cannot be as scary as that floofy bell that keeps—"

Amp didn't finish, because my hand shot out as fast as a frog's tongue, and I snatched up my alien pal.

"I should be drop-kicking you across the blacktop," I growled at the tiny blue head poking out of my fist.

He made a pained face. "Too tight," he managed to bleat. I loosened my grip and he gulped at the air. "I said I was sorry."

"You can't just turn a school upside down because you need some spare parts for your crummy space ship," I said. "Or turn a life upside down."

"I haven't turned anything upside down," he said with a puzzled look.

"You know what I mean," I said with clenched teeth.

"No, I truly don't know what you mean."

"This is a disaster," I hissed. "Olivia's in there trying to get me out of trouble. My whole class thinks I'm a complete nutball. Lexie Evans wants to touch my hair."

He thought about all this for a minute. "You're right, I was not careful with my impulse trick. I won't do it again."

"Thank you," I sighed. But now it was my turn to think about things for a minute. "Not so fast," I said, snapping my fingers. I sat up straight. "Hey, we could use your little mind trick one more time. I'm in a real pickle here."

"Wait, what about a pickle? I didn't follow the pickle part."

"It's a saying."

"A saying?"

"A figure of speech."

"I've spent years learning Earth languages. All of them. And never have I heard that people can be *in* a pickle. Very strange—and dangerous. It seems to me you'd risk being eaten."

"Listen," I said, taking a deep breath. "We need to use your Jedi mind trick thing on Principal Luntz. If he calls my dad, I will be grounded until I'm a grandfather."

"That sounds terrible."

"So just shoot some of those thought-balls in his direction. You know, like how I'm a great kid."

"No, you said not to do that trick anymore. You said my mind trick was turning things upside down. I was wrong to use it. How could using it again be a good thing?"

"My goose is cooked here, Amp. I've painted myself into a corner. I'm hanging by a thread. You get that, right?"

"Something about your goose hanging in a corner," he said with a helpless look on his face. "I'm still trying to figure out the pickle thing."

I groaned. "I know I told you to not do that mind stuff again. I get that. But I want you to make an exception in this case."

He screwed up his little face and looked into the distance. "Let me think about this."

I waited a full minute. "Well?" I finally said.

"I need more time. I'll let you know tomorrow."

"Tomorrow? Are you kidding me? I'm going to get creamed now."

"Zack," Olivia's voice called out as Principal Luntz's door clicked open. "Would you join us in here?"

I hoisted Amp up so we could see eye to eye.

"You are the most frustrating alien in the whole stinkin' universe," I growled, then shoved him back inside my backpack and headed into Principal Luntz's office.

12

Showdown

"**O**livia here tells me you've been sleepwalking," Principal Luntz said, focusing on me through his reading glasses like I was a fly caught between a pair of chopsticks.

"Somnambulism is nothing to be ashamed of," Olivia added.

"Somna . . . what?" I said, sitting down next to Olivia in the empty chair in front of Principal Luntz's desk.

"Olivia is right," Principal Luntz said with a slight smirk. "I understand you've been traipsing about your neighborhood in the middle of the night in your boxers."

"Unmentionables," Olivia corrected him.

"What?" I yelped. I shot Olivia a look. "That's not . . . What the heck does 'traipsing' mean?"

"Look, I'm sure there's medication your parents can get for you," Principal Luntz said.

Medication? I looked at Olivia and raised my eyebrows. She gave me a confident smile in return.

Principal Luntz leaned forward and peered at me over his glasses. "Now then, this business about having a crush on your teacher, Miss Martin. I'm afraid there's no medication for that type of thing."

"Who?" I asked, not understanding what Principal Luntz just said. I whipped my head in Olivia's direction. "What did you—" I stared at Olivia, but she didn't return my gaze.

"Zack, sometimes we have feelings that we don't understand," Principal Luntz said, tapping the tip of his pencil on his nose.

"No!" I interrupted. "I don't have any feelings."

Principal Luntz gave me a calming motion with both hands. "Despite the strong feelings that we have, we still have to comport ourselves with the utmost propriety."

I shook my head. "'Comport'? I'm afraid I have no—"

Olivia grabbed my arm. "What Principal Luntz is saying is that despite the fact you're experiencing a severe case of puppy love, you can't act out inappropriately in class."

"Exactly!" exclaimed Principal Luntz, pointing at Olivia with his pencil.

"Puppy love?" I groaned, staring at Olivia with crazy eyes. "Really?"

"There's nothing to be ashamed of," Principal Luntz said with chuckle.

"Yes, Zack, it's the most natural thing in the world," Olivia said, patting my arm with a pretend look of understanding and sympathy.

"These feelings will pass, probably in a few days," Principal Luntz said with a dramatic wave of his hand. "Nothing to be ashamed of."

"I am not ashamed of anything," I said slowly. "I don't even—"

"But in the meantime let's cool it with the disruptive behavior in class," Principal Luntz interrupted, gazing intently at me over his glasses.

"Okay," I whispered, defeated.

"Wonderful! I must say, Zack, you're lucky to have a friend like Olivia. She is one sharp cookie.

She explained everything. But what really concerns me is the bit about you sleepwalking in your underwear."

"Unmentionables," Olivia corrected him again.

"Unmentionables, yes," he agreed, nodding. Unbelievable.

"That could be dangerous," he said, almost smiling before leaning forward and pressing a button on his phone. We heard a ringing on the speaker. "So, I'll just have Miss Sturney call your mom for me. I'll notify her of the situation and let her decide the best course of action."

Olivia sat up. She looked at me with panic in her eyes. "Oh, I don't think that will be necessary."

"But—" was all I could think to say before Miss Sturney, our school's secretary, answered Principal Luntz on the intercom. "Yes, Mr. Luntz," we heard her say through the small speaker. "What's up?"

At that moment, something strange happened: Principal Luntz opened his mouth to speak, but didn't say anything.

Olivia and I exchanged a look.

"Bob, you still there?" we heard Miss Sturney ask.

And just as quickly as he froze, he came back to life. "Miss Sturney, I feel like a yummy banana split. With walnuts. And some of those colorful little things on top."

Now Olivia and I both froze.

Amp!

"What do you call those little things?" Principal Luntz asked us.

"Do you mean sprinkles?" I said after a moment's pause.

"Yes, sprinkles!" Principal Luntz cried. "You catch that, Miss Sturney?"

The speaker on the intercom was silent. Miss Sturney was obviously processing this odd request. "You want a banana split, right? Well, I've got

lunch orders here, sir, that I have to get to the cafeteria, but I guess I could run out for one—a banana split, I mean—if you really need one."

"With walnuts," Principal Luntz added.

"And sprinkles," I added.

"Yes, I heard you," an unhappy Miss Sturney answered.

Miss Sturney sounded downright peeved. But Principal Luntz looked as happy as a kid on the first day of summer. He released the button on the intercom, cutting off Miss Sturney without so much as a "Thank you."

"Scrumdiddlyumptious!" he said with a giddy chuckle and a clap of his hands. "Okay, now back to class with you both." He scribbled on a yellow pad, and tore off two late passes.

I stood. Olivia stayed put, looking from the late pass to Principal Luntz a few times.

"Olivia," I hissed. I stepped toward her, gently grabbed her wrist, and led her slowly out of Principal Luntz's office. I shut the door without looking back.

"Did you do that banana split thing?" she asked.

I shrugged.

"Dang it, Zack, you need to tell me what's going on, or I'm calling the FBI!"

I looked around. "Okay, okay," I said. "But I can't show you here. C'mon, follow me."

13

The Reveal

Standing in the janitor's supply closet with Olivia, I found myself at a loss for words. Just yesterday I had a good idea of what fourth grade was going to be all about. Now it was about avoiding interplanetary war and dealing with an annoying blue alien who could make you gag on imaginary spoiled milk.

Man, what a difference a day can make.

Olivia folded her arms. Her eyes were drilling through mine. She was waiting for an explanation, and I hadn't the foggiest idea where to start.

"This better be good," she said through clenched teeth.

"You remember that blue guy I was telling you about?"

"Oh, for heaven's sake!" she exploded. "Not

this again. Look, I'm not buying any explanation that involves your imaginary, sad uncle."

"He's not my uncle!" I exploded back.

"Well, then who are you talking about?"

I sat down on a huge, white bucket of floor polish. I placed my backpack on the next bucket, knowing Amp was probably listening to all of this.

"Use your words, Zack," Olivia said.

"Enough of this!" Amp called out from the pocket of my backpack.

Olivia was so taken aback by my backpack's sudden ability to speak, she shrieked, stumbled backward, and fell awkwardly over a mop bucket on wheels. After bouncing off a wobbly shelf of toilet paper, she fell onto her back. The rolls wobbled, tipped over, and tumbled down on top of her.

"Agh!" she cried.

"Olivia!" I rushed over and tossed the toilet paper rolls off of her.

"There's something in your backpack?" she stammered.

I nodded. "I told you he was small. Listen, he won't hurt you. He's my friend. He's nice. He's an alien. And I'm helping him fix his spaceship. Got it?"

Olivia stared at me. "That's a lot of information to give someone all at once."

I helped her sit up, and right there, just five feet in front of her, was Amp. He had crawled out of his pocket and was now standing perfectly still in front of us. He waved and did his best to make a friendly smile, though it really looked more like he had gas.

"It's the bald Smurf from your room this morning," she whispered with a quivery voice. "Is he dangerous?"

"He's a pain in the neck,

but not too dangerous," I said.

"Are you sure?" she said. "He looks weird."

"C'mon, Mr. Jinxy practically ate him. I've almost stepped on him twice."

"You know I can hear you both, right?" Amp asked.

"He sounds ridiculous," she said.

"He's funny, huh?" I agreed, helping her up.

"Is he poisonous?" Olivia asked, not taking her eyes off Amp.

"Poisonous?" I asked with a laugh. "Of course not."

"How do you know?" she asked.

"I'm not dead, am I?" I answered.

"Zack, I watched this old black-and-white movie once with my grandpa called *War of the Worlds*. It was about these aliens who come to Earth. But the aliens all end up dying because of bacteria, which are invisible."

"He's fine!" I protested. "Healthy as a clam!"

"Not him!" she said, grabbing my shoulders and looking at me with wide eyes. "He could have brought something here. Like killer germs or viruses or mold!"

"He's not moldy," I said. "Relax."

"Olivia is correct to be concerned," Amp said, waving his arms to get our attention. "She is a sharp cookie indeed. I'm not sure how 'cookie' and 'sharp' go together, but her fear is logical."

"Wait, you brought mold with you?" I asked.

"I am not like you both," he reassured us. "I don't carry other organisms on my body. Single-celled or otherwise. Totally different biology.

"Council Note,"

he whispered into his wrist again.

"Germs. They are microorganisms, really small living things. Apparently, some of them can make humans sick. Further study warranted."

"What was that about?" Olivia asked.

"Oh, he's studying us," I told her. "His planet is planning to invade Earth."

"What?!" Olivia yelped. "You should have called the president. Or the army. Or an exterminator!"

"Calm down," I said. "Amp is a scout. He came to check things out. Obviously, he's realized that invading Earth is a really bad idea. So he needs to hurry up and get back to call the whole thing off. We've got to help him."

Olivia thought this over. "Am I the first person you've told about him?" she asked, concern now rising in her voice.

"He's my friend, Olivia," I said. "If other people find out, it'll become a mess."

"It's already a mess," Olivia said. "Listen, Zack, that's an alien standing right there. Don't you watch movies? These things always turn out badly!"

"Olivia, I need to return to call off the attack," Amp explained. "The sooner the better. In fact, ideally by four forty this afternoon."

"What!" I shouted. "That's hours away, Amp!"

"That's why I couldn't wait at your house. I need a high-powered magnet and we need to figure out an alternative way to launch my spaceship if I'm going be able to get back to Erde in time."

"Well, so much for calling in the cavalry," Olivia said. "By the time we get the police to believe our

91

story, we'll be serving our Erdian overlords."

"The key thing," Amp explained, "is that my initial launch system needs to be replaced. You could help me and Zack. We could use a sharp cookie like you."

"Oh, and what kind of cookie am I?" I asked Amp.

"I'm sorry, I still don't get the whole cookie connection," Amp said. "I'm just trying to fit in. Look, all I need is to replace my initial launch system. Surely you can help with that?"

"I don't even know what an initial launch whosie-whatsie is, so probably not," Olivia said.

"Well, I need to get my ship moving up, away from this planet, before I can activate my secondary thrusters."

"How about a trampoline?" I said. "Or we could just throw it."

Amp groaned. "It's not a paper airplane, Zack."

"Hey, I'm just spitballing here, Amp! There are no bad ideas when you're spitballing."

"But you just came up with two," he said, looking confused.

Just then the bell rang and Amp dove instantly back into the pocket of my backpack.

"See, he's even scared of a floofy bell," I said, but my voice sounded hollow now. "Okay then, how about this: we'll sneak into the science lab after school." I snatched up my backpack and carefully zipped Amp's pocket. "There has to be something there that we can use. I mean, how hard can it be to launch a spaceship?"

We exited the janitor's closet and headed off to the gym for PE class in a daze.

Olivia sighed. "Honestly, how am I supposed to concentrate on jumping rope now that we're just hours away from preventing an alien invasion of Earth?"

I could not have agreed with her more.

14

Blocked

"**N**o tungsten, but there are magnets here that we need," Amp said.

Olivia and I hid out in a recess equipment supply closet after school finished for the day. Surrounded by scuffed balls, bats, jump ropes, nets, hula hoops, and orange pylons of every description, we listened carefully as Amp described what he needed.

"Hold on. What's a tungsten?" Olivia asked.

"It's a special kind of high-density metal that can resist heat," I explained. I could feel Olivia staring at me with surprise. I wasn't known for my knowledge of rare metals, or anything having to do with science for that matter. "The science lab doesn't have any," I continued. "But it does have magnets, which we also need to fix

Amp's spaceship."

"I'll have to do without the tungsten," Amp said. "It makes my voyage through space more dangerous, but I can go without it."

"How do you know we have the magnets you need?" Olivia asked Amp.

"I checked this morning, during the commotion in the classroom," Amp said.

"Commotion you created," I said.

"Sorry about that," Amp said, actually sounding sorry.

"You only have three fingers," Olivia blurted.

Amp looked at his little hands. "True," he said simply. "Three seems to be plenty. What do you do with your two extra fingers?"

Now it was our turn to look at our hands. It was odd to think of fingers as "extra."

Olivia looked up. "How can you speak English so well if you just got here yesterday?"

"Gosh, Olivia, he's not on trial," I said.

"No, it's a fair question," Amp said to me. "Erdians happen to be quite good at languages. I've learned all the Earth languges. Although complex, yours was not too difficult to figure out, but clearly I still have lots to learn, like why it's good if a cookie is sharp."

Olivia and I thought about that for minute. Neither of us could figure out a way to explain it.

"We have learned the language of many other life-forms from faraway solar systems. Some languages are just simple chemical reactions, but another one we've learned is probably two hundred times more complicated than yours."

"Wait a minute," I said. "What are you saying, Amp? Are you saying you've met other people from other planets?"

"Well, I wouldn't describe them as people," he said casually. "Let's just say they're life-forms. Actually, one is a lot like a cactus plant on this planet. Not surprisingly, they don't have much to say. However, there is one non-carbon-based life-form that is the size of your planet. You should see them. They are big, slimy, blob-type things, but friendly if you get to know them. But it takes them about a year in Earth time to say one full sentence. Frankly, I didn't have the patience."

"We are not alone," I said in my best scary voice.

Olivia rolled her eyes.

I cleared my throat. "Listen to the hallway; it's totally quiet now. We have to get in that lab before Mr. Hoog comes in to clean it."

"Excuse me," Olivia said, "but I'm not sure it's right to just steal stuff from the science lab, spaceship or no spaceship. Stealing is not good."

"I don't know," I said. "Steal some junky old lab magnets or let the planet be attacked by an army of three-fingered blue aliens? Seems like a no-brainer."

"I'm just saying," Olivia said, folding her arms.

"There are lots of magnets in the lab," Amp said. "But there is one type in particular that I'm interested in. It's made of neodymium, iron, and boron. Each of those is on that big poster of elements in the lab, Zack."

"I remember," I said with a nod.

Amp continued like a half-pint professor. "The neodymium magnets have a very strong magnetic field. Very stable. They are so strong they could be dangerous, but the ones in your lab are quite small. No bigger than my hand. Very safe and perfect for what we need."

"But we can't just steal them from the school," Olivia said. "They're not ours. They belong to the school."

Amp nodded. "I only need one to reset a few instruments on my ship, the ones that help me navigate as I skip through space. Twenty minutes is all I need. So let's not steal it, let's just borrow it without asking. We can return it tomorrow."

"Okay, we're in," Olivia said. "But if we get caught, our noodles are cooked."

"I have no idea what that means," Amp said.

"That's exactly what worries us," Olivia said, reading the look on my face.

15

Borrowing
(without Asking)

It was as if the stars had aligned.

And all the planets.

And a few asteroids, too.

Everything was going as planned.

The school's main corridor was a ghost town. Not a sign of Mr. Hoog. No teachers walking around. No kids goofing off waiting to be picked up.

We reached the lab absolutely, categorically, and unbelievably unseen.

I raised myself up and peered through the lab door's small window. The room was dark and quiet and empty. I grabbed the door's handle, took a deep breath, and turned it. It was open!

"Piece of cake," I said, reminding myself not to switch on the lights.

"Let's do this, little man," Olivia said to Amp,

who was hanging out of the backpack slung over my shoulder.

"The magnets we need are in that tub, on top of that white cabinet," Amp said from behind me.

"Whoa, that's high," I said, seeing the plastic tub labeled MAGNETS, BATTERIES, MARBLES, & DOMINOES.

"The robot club must have had a party in here," Olivia said. There were several half-assembled robots on one of the lab tables next to a box labeled ROBOT PARTS. There were also plates of half-eaten cookies, a bowl of cheese balls, a platter of M&Ms, and assorted two-liter soda bottles and cups standing everywhere on the table. "Your brother and his robot-nerd friends are slobs."

I dragged a tall lab stool over to the cabinet. It made a loud screeching sound.

Olivia, who was now tossing M&Ms in the air and catching them in her mouth, said, "Gosh, Zack, why don't you shoot off some fireworks while you're at it."

"Sorry, sorry, sorry," I said, dropping my backpack onto the lab table in front of the cabinet. "But c'mon, Olivia, we only have about an hour to save the world from Amp's . . . friends."

I climbed up and stood on the stool. I reached up to the tub with the magnets and yanked it off the shelf with all my strength. Unfortunately, it wasn't as heavy as I thought. I wobbled and started to fall backward off the stool. I had to drop the tub behind me or I was going to fall backward and break my neck. "Amp!" I shouted. "Look out!"

The tub crashed onto the lab table with a hideous cracking sound, almost flattening a terrified Amp, who had crawled out to watch me borrow a magnet.

The tub split into two parts. Magnets, batteries, marbles, and dominoes shot off in every direction. Several plastic soda bottles went bouncing crazily across the table, sending stale chips and cheese balls into the air in what can be best described as a junk food explosion. I watched with wide eyes as three of the spinning soda bottles flew off the table.

"ZACK!" Olivia screamed.

Apparently the slobs in the robot club didn't bother to tighten the caps of their bottles either, because now the shaken-up soda came spurting out of the tops.

The grape soda bottle whizzed around in a circle and showered a stunned Olivia with huge purple dots.

The root beer bottle hissed for an instant and shot straight across the floor, hitting Skip the Skeleton in his unmentionable area. Skip leaned dangerously forward, like he was about to jump over a creek. Then, to my horror, Skip's neck broke, leaving just his skull dangling.

The still-fizzing two-liter root beer bottle was on the floor, trapped up in Skip's rib cage.

As the fizzing petered out, the room got eerily quiet.

The lab was now covered in cheese balls, M&Ms, stale chips, plastic cups, magnets, batteries, marbles, dominoes, bones, soda slime, and empty bottles.

"That could have gone better," Amp said quietly.

"What just happened?" Olivia whispered,

holding her dripping arms out to the side. For a second I thought she was crying, but it was just grape soda dripping down her face.

"I'm think I'm going to jail for the rest of my life," I squeaked.

16

What a Blast

Olivia finally broke the silence. "That was awesome," she said, looking around the now destroyed science lab.

She walked over to an empty bottle and picked it up. "The cap split open," she said, "which must be why the soda fizzed out like that."

"Are you crazy?" I yelped, still standing on my stool. "We killed Skip!"

"Skip's a skeleton. He was already a goner," Olivia said, lifting his head up for a moment to look him in the eye sockets.

"Excuse me, but I think your Mr. Hoog is coming this way," Amp said. "He must have heard the commotion."

"My life is over," I whispered.

"This way!" Amp shouted. "We need to escape!"

He headed for the emergency exit at the back of the lab, which opened onto the playground.

"Aren't we going to clean this place up?" I croaked.

"They'll just think the robot club made this mess," Olivia hissed. "Besides, we don't have time. Remember?"

"What about our fingerprints?" I said. "They must be everywhere."

"You watch too much TV," Olivia said.

"We really should go now," Amp warned us, picking up one of the magnets off the floor and waving it at us.

Olivia took the broken cap off the bottle and tossed it on the floor. She reached into a container of black rubber stoppers and found one that fit the bottle. "Hey, maybe we could use this to launch Amp's ship—sorta like the booster rocket they use on the space shuttle." She shook the bottle and the soda fizzed up again. "What do you think?"

"I think I'm going to be sent to a camp for troubled youth," I said.

"You're overly dramatic," Olivia said.

"GUYS!" Amp shouted in an even higher pitch than usual. "NOW!"

Olivia ran for the door. I followed her through the door.

"WAIT!" I had forgotten my backpack on the lab table!

I spun and grabbed the door just before it locked me out. I dashed across hundreds of cheese balls, crunch-crunching the whole way, and grabbed my backpack just as I heard Mr. Hoog's keys jangling on the other side of the door. In a matter of seconds, I made it back out the door, scooped up Amp, hid him in my backpack, and took off after Olivia across the school's soccer field.

We squeezed through a hole in the gate at the back of the school and ran next to a dry creek alongside the back of the school.

We jogged for half a mile or so. After cutting across an old muddy field, we reached our street. Olivia spoke for the first time. "I've been thinking," she gasped.

"Oh no," I said, pressing my palms onto my knees as I tried to catch my breath.

"No, seriously," she said, hitting me with the

soda bottle. "If we can get the fizz to come out really strong, the bottle will fly into the air. It could launch Amp's ship."

"But how do we force the air in and the fizz out the bottom?"

"We poke a hole in the stopper," she suggested, "and we shake up the soda so that it's super fizzy."

I thought about that for a second. "I don't think

that'll be enough force to push Amp's ship into the air. It's pretty small and not very heavy, but still . . ."

We both stood there thinking about it. I couldn't think of anything. Apparently, Olivia was stumped, too.

"We'll think of something," she said.

"The sooner the better," I said, not thinking of anything yet.

"In the meantime, I'll make a hole in the stopper," she said, jogging off. "I'll meet you in your backyard in ten minutes," she called back over her shoulder.

"Hurry," I said, focusing on the task in front of us and already forgetting about the mess we had made back at the school's lab. "We have exactly forty-five minutes to save the world!"

17

Smart Stuff

The more I thought about blasting Amp's ship into the air, the more nervous I became.

Amp was encouraged when I told him about our idea, but he was also distracted with worry, mumbling to himself as he punched numbers into a small calculator-looking device that he had pulled from his belt. He also sent about ten "Council Notes" off, each one sounding more and more worried. For the last one, I overheard him say:

"Council Note: Propulsion. It means creating enough force to cause movement. Gravity. It is the Earth force that holds me to the ground. I am going to try, but I fear the propulsion from this experiment

is not going to be nearly strong enough to overcome gravity. If I don't make into orbit, please have someone water my plants at home."

We waited for Olivia to come back, and Amp tried resetting a device on his spaceship with the magnet he had picked up from the classroom floor. He shouted what sounded like Erdian curse words a few times and huffed off into the house. He emerged moments later with his helmet on, looking slightly more optimistic.

And while he was doing that, I thought about that bottle. The fizzing soda didn't seem to be powerful enough to lift Amp's ship into space. Not to mention how we'd keep the soda in if we used a stopper with a hole in it. And that's when an idea danced into my brain: What if we jammed air into the bottle, like with a straw, until it was ready to burst? That would increase the pressure in the bottle, so soda would shoot out the bottom. It would also keep the soda in until we were ready to release it.

I looked at Amp. He was shaking his head. "What?" I said.

"Keep thinking," he said, nervously adjusting his tool belt.

The straw probably wasn't the ideal strategy. That might work for a balloon to fly around the room, but if you're building a rocket it's just not enough energy, or power, or force, or whatever.

"Ready for takeoff?" Olivia said from behind me. Her head was poking through a break in the fence between our houses. "Check it out," she said handing me the bottle. "The hole is tiny."

I looked at the stopper and started to violently shake the bottle as hard as I could.

"What are you doing?" Olivia asked.

I quickly turned the bottle over and looked at the stopper. The soda left in the bottle had gotten all foamy, but just fizzy drips were coming out the hole. "See, this isn't going to work," I said. "We need more air in there. Like a ton of air. I was thinking of using a straw."

"That'll never work," she said, looking at me with half-closed eyes.

113

"I know," I said. We both stood staring at the bottle.

"Are you helping, or just watching?" Olivia asked when she noticed Amp watching us. "Hey, nice hat."

"It's a helmet," Amp said, offended.

Olivia slapped her thigh. "Well? Can you throw us a bone here, spaceman, before your people show up and start shooting up the place?"

"Oh, that would not be good," Amp said distractedly. He seemed to remember something, and started tapping again on his calculator.

"What's his problem? There's no time for math," Olivia said, turning back to me. "If we could just pump air inside this thing . . ."

"Wait as second!" I shouted. "That's it. A pump! My bike pump! I have a needle thing I use to pump up my basketball."

"That could work," Olivia said. "Go get it, dude! We're at T minus thirty and counting."

In less than a minute, I was pumping air into that bottle like a madman. The bike pump's needle just cleared the end of the stopper inside the bottle. At first, the stopper popped off before

much air got it, so I removed the needle and pushed the stopper in as hard as I could. Then I pushed the needle back in and we took turns pumping.

Air bubbles rose up through the soda and the bottle became hard as steel.

We set the bottle on the outdoor wooden table. I slowly pulled the needle out, but once it cleared the stopper nothing happened. "I thought something would come out of the hole," I said.

"Let me pull the stopper out," Olivia said.

"Wait!" I shouted, but it was too late. Olivia was blasted with fizzing soda and the bottle shot across the table right at my stomach. I barely managed to jerk out of its way.

It flew several feet in the air then skidded across the cement. It hit a big planter with a small lemon tree in it and spun around wildly several times, making a loud *pshhhhhht* sound, spraying soda everywhere.

It had only lasted a few seconds, but Olivia and I jumped around like we had just won a million dollars in the lottery. We both gave Amp a high five—or a high three in his case.

Soon, we settled down and stared at the now resting bottle.

"Great, but now we're out of soda," Olivia said.

"No worries. We just need some quick adjustments," I said. I filled the bottle all the way up with water from the hose.

"Really?" Olivia said.

"You two do know what you're doing, right?" Amp asked. "Remember that I am the one who'll be blasting off."

"Of course," I said. "It's all about the air pressure," I added confidently, pumping air into the bottle I'd filled almost completely with water. The pressure rose till the stopper finally popped out, and that one barely made it off the edge of table.

"Wonderful," Amp sighed.

"All part of the

process," I smiled, knowing full well that science was all about trial and error. "I guess that one was way too heavy to launch."

I filled the bottle halfway with water. Then I pumped while Olivia held the sides, pointing the rocket straight up from the table. That was much better, going almost ten feet into the air, but it still lacked the oomph we needed.

"I have an idea," Olivia said. She filled the bottle with just a cup of water and did all the pumping while I did the holding, leaning away so the bottle wouldn't hit me in the face. That one finally popped off on its own, but it was a dud.

"Okay, one-third full must be just right, Goldi-locks," I said, "like the first time in the lab."

"Okay, Baby Bear, but we still have a few more tweaks to make. And we better hurry, because it must be at least four fifteen by now."

"Time waits for no alien," I declared.

18

Launch

"These should help shoot the rocket straight up and let us launch from a safer distance," Olivia said, pounding a fourth wooden stake into the grass with a croquet mallet.

We had agreed that in order for our bottle rocket to shoot straight up, it needed some wings, like the rockets in the movies. That was my job. I had cut cardboard fins out of an old shoebox and was in the process of carefully taping them to the sides of our bottle. "This looks totally wicked," I said.

"Kind of messy, though," Olivia said, looking at my taping job. "C'mon, Zack, this isn't rocket science."

"Ha, ha, ha," I said. "Maybe I'll tape you to this rocket and blast you to the moon."

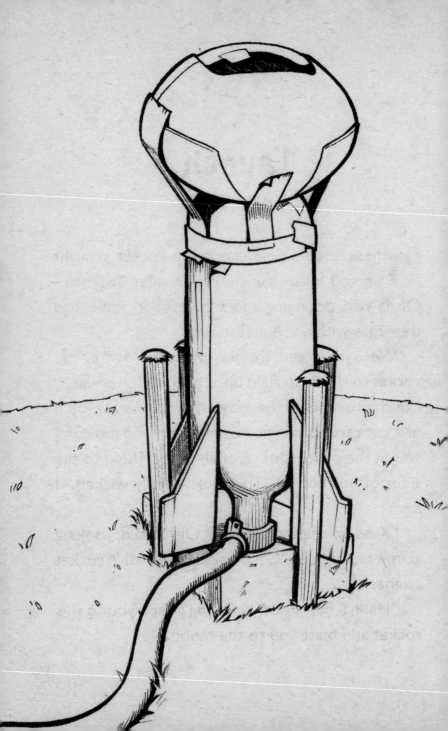

I picked up a small square cement brick out of the dirt near my mom's rosebushes and dropped it inside the four stakes on the grass. "Our launch-pad," I said proudly.

We got some fresh root beer from my refrigerator and poured it slowly into the rocket with a funnel until it was about a third full. Olivia shoved in the black stopper and I pushed in the pump needle.

We carefully placed the bottle on the launch-pad, stepped back, and nodded for a few seconds, admiring our own handiwork.

"Okay," Olivia said, turning to Amp, "let's go get your ship."

"Already?" he said, speaking for the first time in a while. He looked less blue, like his color was fading. He was chewing on his finger.

"You look terrible, Amp," Olivia said.

"I'm a little nervous," he squeaked.

"It's four twenty-five, Amp," I explained. "We only have fifteen minutes to get you up there."

"How high will it lift me?" he asked, looking up nervously.

I shrugged. "I'm not sure. Pretty high."

"This is not how we do things on Erde," he said.

"Look, Amp, this is the best two kids from Earth can whip together in an afternoon," I said. "It's now or never, little guy. Are you a hero or a zero? "

He nodded and adjusted his helmet. "Okay, Zack, bring down my ship."

I sprinted upstairs and carried down Amp's spaceship. Olivia held it in place as I secured it to our rocket with the same packing tape I had used for the wings.

"It hardly weighs anything," Olivia marveled. "So weird."

I ran inside to check the clock on the kitchen stove. "It's four thirty-five!" I shouted. "We're out of time. Prepare for blastoff!"

Amp jumped into the palm of my hand. He had his game face on. He still looked a few shades lighter than he should, but he was ready.

"Good luck," I said, giving Amp a high three.

Olivia did the same. "Happy trails, squirt," she said.

I placed Amp inside his ship. The door closed

tight, and before I could step back it started whirring, clicking, and hissing steam out of its tiny holes.

"Whoa," Olivia said, jumping back. "That is crazy cool."

I picked up the snorkeling mask I had found while searching for the bike pump in the garage and snapped it over my face. I shoved the snorkel's mouthpiece into my mouth. "Retha," I mumbled.

"You look ridiculous," Olivia said.

"Leth do thith." I said, smiling as best I could.

19

We Have Liftoff

I tried my best not to think about the fact that the fate of the universe now rested on a rocket Olivia and I had built in about the time it takes to broil a chicken.

Instead, I focused my mind on pushing the last of the air into the bottle before launch. It was so hard to pump, I thought my arms might blast off before the rocket did.

"All clear for takeoff, Rocket One," Olivia announced unsteadily. "All systems go. Five, four, three, two, one . . . BLAST OFF!"

I leaned on the pump, forcing a last tiny gurgle of air bubbles into the straining bottle.

"BLAST OFF!" Olivia screamed, kicking me in the foot.

"Ith thtuck!" I mumbled through the snorkel's

mouthpiece, straining to keep my weight over the pump handle.

"ZACK, WE'RE GOING TO BE TOO LATE! WE'RE OUT OF TIME! DO SOMETHING!"

I gasped, yanked the handle up for one more push, and practically gave myself the Heimlich maneuver as I threw my whole body weight onto the pump, stomach-first. One tiny bubble emerged through the needle into the root beer. And then:

PSHSHSHSTTT!

My goggles were suddenly covered with soda foam, and the rocket in front of me had disappeared. My face was soaked. I fell off the pump onto my back and watched our rocket shoot straight into the air above me, turning just slightly as it soared perfectly skyward.

It had worked!

Through the goggles, I saw the slowly shrinking bottle easily clear our second-story roof and continue into the sky. But then it slowed and seemed to stick in the air. It hung there for what felt like three seconds, but nothing happened.

The nose of the rocket—Amp's ship— tipped over back toward Earth, and the whole

taped-together contraption fell slowly back down to the lawn, a trail of leftover soda leaking out of it as it fell.

Amp's ship hit the grass about fifty feet from where it'd taken off from with an unspectacular thud.

Olivia and I stared in silence.

"Amp, are you still alive in there?" Olivia called out in a whisper.

We waited, breaths held.

Then the door of the spaceship slid open and Amp poked his tiny blue head out. "That was not high enough," he reported matter-of-factly.

Olivia and I both gasped in relief that he was still alive.

But then the reality of situation hit me and I spit out the snorkel's mouthpiece. "That means the invasion force is launching from Erde right now?"

"Yeah, about that," he said sheepishly. "Funny thing there. As I was being launched into the air by your very impressive piece of engineering here, I realized my calculations were incorrect."

"What's that mean?" I croaked.

He pulled his little calculator device out of his belt. "I remembered that this device calculates what time it is based on its current location, which of course right now is your planet."

Olivia and I looked at each other, not understanding.

Amp cleared his throat. "A day on Earth is much shorter than a day on my planet."

"How much shorter?" I finally thought to ask.

"Let me see. I just need to manually override the settings. Give or take a few minutes, because I haven't figured it out down to the second yet, I think we actually have about 119 days."

"Are you kidding me?" Olivia roared. "I almost had a heart attack, Amp."

"A hundred nineteen days . . ." I moaned, falling onto my back and staring up at the blue sky through my still-soaked snorkeling mask. "Amp, I swear I'd strangle you if I weren't completely exhausted."

I couldn't help but start laughing, which spread to Olivia, and finally to Amp, who I'm convinced wasn't sure why he was laughing—he was just trying to fit in.

Lying there on the damp grass, I felt proud and relieved at the same time, knowing that I had launched an actual rocket and that my odd little friend from another planet wouldn't be leaving us quite so soon.

20

In the Catbird S

You would think the son who had an alien invader secretly stashed in his bedroom and had just caused a jaw-dropping mess at his elementary school would be the topic of conversation at dinner that night.

I wasn't.

Taylor was.

"Tell me again, son," my dad said to Taylor, "I thought you and the boys in the robot club normally clean up after your meetings. What happened?"

"We usually do, Dad," Taylor said, picking at his mashed potatoes with his electric fork. "We left a few things on the table, sure, but it wasn't a big deal."

"Not according to Mr. Hoog," my mom said sternly. "The email we got from Principal Luntz

131

was very critical of the robot club. Poor Mr. Hoog is probably still there mopping up."

"So weird," Taylor mumbled, mystified how a few cups and bottles became the worst mess in elementary school history.

"I, for one, am also disappointed, little brother," I said, enjoying not being in the hot seat for once.

My dad shot me his patented mad-dad look, but he didn't say anything.

After a moment of quiet, I spoke up. "Speaking of the lab, some of the magnets in there are neodymium magnets," I announced. "They're a really strong, stable, permanent magnet. They're actually an alloy made up of neodymium, iron, and boron. Those are elements, in case you didn't already know."

My dad looked up from his steak and stared at me like *I* was the alien in the house. Even Taylor looked up from his mashed potatoes.

"What just happened?" my mom asked, looking around the table.

"Zack knows something I don't know," Taylor answered glumly. "The whole world is upside down."

"Wow, Zack," my dad said. "This year really is going to be different, isn't it?"

"Oh, it's different already," I said, popping a string bean in my mouth.

"Use your utensils, honey," Mom said. "Germs."

"I heard you and Olivia made a rocket and shot it off in the backyard." My dad chuckled with amazement.

"Oh, dear, that sounds dangerous," my mom said.

"We were super careful," I said. "I even wore a mask."

My dad turned to Taylor. "Looks like we might have more than one young scientist at this

table—a rocket scientist, no less."

Taylor groaned and went back to re-mashing his potatoes.

"Oh, Mom and Dad," I said, "do you two know anything about tungsten? It's an element. It's the W on the periodic table. Atomic weight of seventy-four. It has a super-high melting point. Carbon is the only element with a higher melting point. Anyway, do you think we might be able to get some?"

The room got so quiet I could almost hear my food being digested.

Suddenly my dad started laughing, like I had just done the most amazing card trick in history. My mom started clapping with excitement. Taylor just held his face in his hands.

"Why on earth would you want that?" my mom asked excitedly.

"Just curious, I guess," I said. "About science and stuff."

"I know next to nothing about how much tungsten costs," my dad said. "But I think we can look it up on the internet."

"If it's safe," my mom added. "We don't want it in the house if it's radioactive."

"It's not radioactive," Taylor said from between his hands.

At that point, my mom jumped up from her chair and came over and gave me a big hug and a couple of kisses on the cheek.

"Nice work, Zack," I heard Amp say inside my head. "You are a very sharp cookie, my friend. Now finish eating. We have more work to do!"

I couldn't help but smile, knowing that this year just might be better—or at least more interesting—than I could have ever imagined.

THE END

Try It Yourself: Bottle Rocket Blastoff

Rockets work by pushing exhaust downward (really fast), which pushes the rocket upward (really fast). You can build your own bottle rocket that uses air pressure to push water downward out of the rocket, which will propel the rocket upward for a big launch.

YOU WILL NEED: 2-liter soda bottle, cardboard, duct tape, a bicycle pump with a pressure gauge, an inflation needle, a rubber stopper, and some stakes.

Building Your Rocket

1. Make sure the rubber stopper can be inserted into the end of the soda bottle so it holds air inside. You can check for a seal by squeezing the bottle when the stopper is pushed in.

2. With the help of an adult, drill a small hole through the stopper so that when you push the inflation needle in, it fits tightly. Try starting with a smaller drill bit than you think you'll need, and redrill the hole bigger later if you really need to. The goal is to have the rubber tight around the needle, making a good seal.

3. Push the inflation needle through the rubber stopper till the end pokes out a little bit. The end with the small hole should be poking out of the smaller tapered end of the stopper.

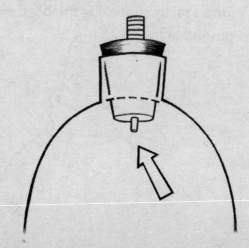

4. Add fins and a nose cone to your bottle to turn it into a rocket! You can design them however you want. Putting the fins near the rocket's nozzle will help it go straight.

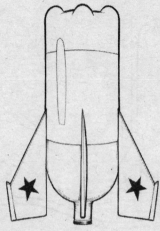

5. Build a launchpad by driving some stakes or sticks into the ground so that your rocket can sit upright while you're pumping the air in.

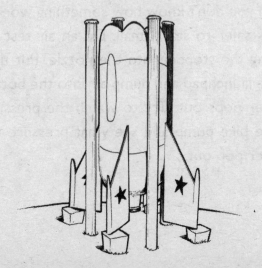

6. Attach the bike pump's nozzle to the inflation needle that's now going through the stopper. Now we're ready to fly!

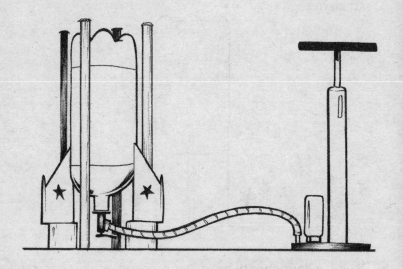

Launch Sequence

1. When you don't know how something works yet, it's always safer to start small. Do an air test by gently pushing the stopper into the nozzle. Put the rocket on the launchpad and pump air into the bottle till the stopper pops out. Try to watch the pressure gauge on the bike pump and see what pressure made the stopper pop out.

2. Do a second air test by pushing the stopper into the rocket nozzle with a little bit more force than last time. Put the rocket back on the pad and pump again till the stopper pops out. You may see a little launch this time, and it should have taken more pressure than last time to force the stopper out. Cool! All systems are "go" for launch.

3. Put some water in the bottle, push the stopper back in, stand back, and start pumping! This time, the rocket should get at least a little launch if the pressure was around 10 PSI or higher before the stopper popped out. Now your rocket works; it's time to do some experiments!

Experiment Time

1. Try varying the amount of force you use to insert the stopper each time. What happens when you push it in very lightly versus with more force? How does it change the pressure required for a launch?

2. Change the amount of water you put in the rocket for each launch. What other important property of the rocket changes when you add lots of water versus a little bit?

3. Test out some different nose cones. Does the rocket fly better with a big, long nose cone that's heavy? How about a short one that uses less material?
4. Vary the size and placement of the fins. What would you need to do to make the rocket spin on its way up?

Tips

- When you're trying to learn about something by changing things, it's important to only change one thing at a time so you can see what a difference it made. That means if you're trying out different nose cones, try to use the same amount of water and air pressure for each launch. That way, if the rocket's flight changes from trial to trial, you know it's because of the different nose cone and not something else.

- If you think you have an idea that explains how something works, think of ways to test out if that idea is true! Do you think that the air pressure is related to how high the rocket flies? How would you test that out?

- Be patient with yourself! When you're trying something new, it might not work right the first or second or third time you try it. Maybe even more times than that. Learn by making observations about the rocket's performance so you can make the right adjustments as you proceed.

Safety Notes

- Rockets store and release a lot of energy! Always make sure that if the rocket were to launch when you don't expect it to, it won't hit anything or anybody that's nearby.
- Make sure everybody around knows that you're going to launch when you're pumping air into the rocket. Doing a countdown helps, especially if you know how many pumps it takes to launch your rocket.
- If you've pumped a lot of air into the rocket and the pressure is high but the rocket's not launching, don't go up to the rocket and try to pull the stopper out. It might launch before you're ready and hit you! Instead, wait till the pressure dies down and reinsert the stopper with less force than you used last time.

Read a sneak peek of book two of the Alien in My Pocket series:

The Science UnFair

Amp sat on the alarm clock I kept next to my bed. My mom was waiting downstairs to drive me to school. The time on the clock told me I had missed the bus fifteen minutes ago and would probably be late for school. I also hadn't finished my homework, and I didn't have an experiment for the science fair yet. So really, being late was the least of my worries.

"Listen, Amp, I have a D in science right now," I said with as much patience as I could muster. "Miss Martin told us—"

"What's the D stand for?" he interrupted.

"It stands for . . . ," I began, trying to remember what the D stood for. "I can't remember! The D stands for disaster, okay! Or dummy! Or dimwit! It doesn't matter what it stand for. It's bad!"

"If it stands for bad, it should be a B, not a D," he said.

"No, a B is good," I said.

"Good should be a G then, right?"

"Gosh dang it, Amp!" I howled. "You can't change the grading system that's been around since my parents were kids. You're missing the main point."

"Hey, I have a great idea for a science experiment."

"Oh, yeah?" I said nervously. A great science fair experiment would definitely help my grade. "What?"

"I'd need some special equipment, of course, and I'd need to sequence a sample of your DNA, but growing a third arm would be really interesting, and easier than you think."

I stared at him. He was either clueless or intentionally trying to make me angry. I could never tell which. "I can't grow another arm!" I shouted. "None of my shirts would fit."

"But you'd be a heck of a juggler," he said softly.

"I can put you in a hamster cage, you know," I said.

"Okay," he said, holding up both hands in surrender. "I'm just asking that you think about it."

I grabbed my head and squeezed it, which, surprisingly, helped me remember something. I jumped up and pulled my science textbook out of my backpack and flipped through the pages. There were twenty or so suggestions for classroom experiments in the glossary in the back. One caught my eye. It showed a potato with a bunch of wires stuck in it and a small lightbulb that was lit up next to it. It was labeled POTATO BATTERY. All I'd need was a potato, some wires, and a lightbulb. How hard could that be?

"Easy," I announced. "I'm going to make a battery out of a potato."

I dropped the book on my bed and pointed to the two photos.

Amp leaped onto the bed and stepped onto the open page. He read in silence. Studied the photos for a minute, stroking his tiny blue chin the whole time.

"Seems kind of dull," he said.

"No, it seems easy. A simple potato battery is perfect."

"Whoa, someone didn't brush his teeth this morning," Amp said, waving his hand in front of his face.

"Funny," I said. "That's what I'm making."

"Fine, but I should warn you that—"

Just then my door popped open and my mom stuck her head in.

I whipped my head in Amp's direction.

But Amp was gone. I looked around, but, thankfully, he had vanished. Mom hadn't noticed. He really was the fastest thing I had ever seen—or not seen.

"Who on earth are you talking to up here?"

"I'm . . . . I'm practicing my science fair presentation," I said weakly.

"You're still doing your homework, Zack?" She sighed. "C'mon, I need to get to work. Better fix that hair first, honey." She headed back down the hallway.

"One second, Mom," I called after her.

"Between her popping in all the time and your brother snooping around, I'm getting nervous about being discovered."

I froze. "What? Taylor's been in here? Looking around? Has he seen you?"

"No, because I usually make myself invisible. Would you like me to tell you how?"

"No, I don't care how. We just can't get caught. If someone sees you they'll take you away, Amp. Then you'll never get home."

Amp looked concerned. "One of these days our luck will run out, Zack. I think your brother is suspicious. We need to get my spaceship repaired!"

"We will, Amp. As soon as I get through this science fair. I can only handle one disaster at a time."